The Fairy Penguin

Tilda Kelly

Contents

Chapter One

Millie Armstrong coloured in the carrot nose on her drawing of a snowman and then added a red-breasted robin, sitting on his shoulder. The other kids on her table were all chatting about their plans for the upcoming summer holidays as they drew their Christmas cards, but Millie didn't join in. She'd only started at Oak Hill Primary School two months ago and she still felt shy around everyone.

I wish we still lived in England, she thought wistfully, looking at the other cards – Santa in red shorts on a surfboard; a Christmas tree with a kangaroo on top instead of an angel; a koala dressed as an elf. No one else had drawn a picture with snow or ice. In Australia, Christmas happened in the summer when the days were long and hot and people celebrated by having barbecues – or barbies – on the beach. It felt so wrong to Millie. It should be cold in December with frosty night skies, roaring fires, mugs of hot chocolate and people wearing warm jumpers, woolly hats and thick coats.

She wondered what her best friend, Lola, was doing to get ready for Christmas in England. A wave of sadness hit her. She and Lola had been best friends since they started school. They tried to keep in touch with video calls but it was hard because southern Australia was eleven hours ahead of

England so a lot of the time when Millie was awake, Lola was in bed! Last time they'd spoken – at the weekend – Lola had sounded really envious when she'd heard that Millie was about to break up for a six-week summer holiday.

"We only get two weeks off for Christmas," she'd said. "It's not fair. I wish I was in Australia!"

Millie sighed. Having a long summer holiday was going to be far less fun with no friends to hang round with. She opened her card and wrote a message inside:

Merry Christmas, Dad.

Love, Millie xxx

Her heart twisted.

Ella, who sat next to her, noticed what she was writing. "Why are you just doing it to your dad and not your mum as well?" she asked.

Alice, on the other side of Ella, elbowed her in the ribs. "Ella!" she hissed, frowning.

Ella's eyes widened. "Oops. Sorry!" she said to Millie. "I forgot about your mum."

"It's OK," said Millie. She fixed her eyes on her card and concentrated on drawing a holly leaf next to the kisses. Her mum had died six months ago, which was why she and her dad had moved to Australia. Her mum had grown up there before moving to England in her twenties. When Millie's mum had passed away after a long illness, Nana, her mum's mother, had suggested Dad and Millie come and live with her on her organic sheep farm in Victoria.

Dad had jumped at the chance for a fresh start but Millie knew Australia would never be home to her. Home was England and always would be.

Ella got up to fetch some glue and Alice leaned across the desk. "I really like your card," she said softly. "Does it always snow lots in England at Christmas time?"

"No," Millie muttered. But then she was sorry. Alice was nice and Millie knew she was trying to be friendly because she felt bad about what Ella had said. She gave her a quick smile. "More than it does here though!"

Alice grinned back. "That's not hard. I bet it's going to be really different for you having Christmas in the summer this year. Are you coming to the barbie on Boxing Day? Everyone meets up on the beach and goes surfing or boogie boarding. It's great fun. I'll be there, well, provided Sasha – that's my dog – isn't having her puppies."

"Puppies?" echoed Millie, looking

at Alice with sudden interest. She loved animals. "Oh, wow! That's really exciting."

"I know. She's due around Boxing Day. The vet scanned her and she's having five pups. She's a kelpie."

"My nana's dog is a kelpie too—" Millie began eagerly but she broke off as Ella came back and plonked herself down between them.

Ella turned to Alice. "So, are you still coming to mine for a sleepover tomorrow, Als? We've got to celebrate the start of the summer holidays!"

Alice nodded and Ella started talking about all the plans she had for their sleepover. Not having been invited, Millie couldn't join in, so she concentrated on finishing her card. When it was done, she put it on the shelf to dry, along with everyone else's. It looked strange next to the pictures of Santa on the beach – out of place and different. *Just like me,* Millie thought with a sigh. Her first Christmas without Mum, in a completely new country with no friends.

No, she really wasn't looking forward to it at all.

After school, everyone in school went to the town centre to sing carols. But they weren't the carols Millie was used to singing. Some were completely new to her, others she thought she knew but as she started to sing them it turned out that they had different words in Australia. *Jingle Bells* wasn't about riding in a sleigh, instead it was about Santa going to the beach in his ute.

After a few people giggled at her when she sang the wrong words, Millie gave up singing out loud and just pretended to sing. She caught sight of her dad and Nana coming through the shopping centre to join the audience. Dad was in a suit after his day in the office – he was an accountant. Nana was in her farm clothes as usual – knee-length khaki shorts, a checked red shirt over a dark blue T-shirt and boots. Her greying hair was pulled back in a stubby ponytail that stuck out through the gap in the back of her faded green baseball cap. Her tanned skin was as wrinkled as an old apple despite the sun cream she applied every day, but her blue eyes were bright and sharp and her arms and legs were lean and strong.

"Hey, Millie!' she called, waving with both hands over her head. "Over here, kid!"

Millie blushed. She gave a tiny wave of her own and quickly looked away. Her grandmother could be quite loud and

a bit embarrassing at times.

"How are you doing?" said Nana, striding over when the carols finished.

"OK," said Millie, aware of the kids around her, chatting all about their plans for after the carol concert. One group was going to the ice cream parlour, another to the juice bar. It made her feel even more lonely. "Shall we go?"

"Not yet," said Nana. "You've still got to see Santa." She nodded to where a man dressed up as Santa Claus was giving out presents to everyone who had been singing carols.

"It's OK. I don't mind not seeing him," said Millie quickly. She didn't feel like talking to Santa, she just wanted to get back to the farm.

"No, come on, I'll get a photo of you with him," said Dad, running a hand through his crinkly brown hair. It was the same chestnut colour as Millie's wavy locks. "We can send it to everyone back in England."

Millie reluctantly let herself be led over to Santa. Nana nudged her forward when it was her turn.

"G'day," said Santa with a smile.

Millie forced herself to smile back. "Um . . . hi."

"So, what do you want for Christmas?"

Millie swallowed. What she wanted was

her mum back but she couldn't say that.
"I . . . I'm not sure."

"There must be something you want,"
said Santa. "What's your Christmas wish,
kiddo?"

Millie saw a group of girls from her
class heading out of the shopping centre,
their arms linked. "To be less lonely," she
whispered.

She spoke too quietly for Santa to

hear. "What was that?" he asked.

"It doesn't matter," Millie said, sighing. "I don't have a Christmas wish."

Santa handed her the present. "Reckon I'll just have to surprise you then. Have a great Christmas!"

Millie nodded. But somehow she doubted that was going to happen.

Chapter Two

"Cock-a-doodle-doo!"

Millie groaned and pulled her pillow over her head as Robert the rooster crowed outside her bedroom window. He woke up every morning just as it was getting light and each day that seemed to be earlier and earlier. Millie shut her eyes and tried to go back to sleep but it was no use. Robert crowed again and then a kookaburra started to make its cackling cry in the gum tree outside. She could hear Nana's loud voice in the yard and Akuna, her dog, barking eagerly as Nana gave him his breakfast. Mornings on the farm always started early.

Millie didn't want to get up. She couldn't remember ever having felt like this on the first day of the summer holidays. If she'd been back in England she'd have jumped out of bed and pulled on her clothes ready to meet up with Lola or spend a day with her mum. Her mum had been a vet and she'd always

tried to arrange her shifts so she could
spend much of the holidays with Millie
doing fun things – swimming and picnics
in the summer, ice skating and going to
the cinema in the winter.

*What am I going to do for the next six
weeks?* Millie thought. Blue Gum Farm
was very isolated; it backed on to a
national park on one side and the coast
on the other. The only way to get to it
was by car. Dad would be out at work
most of the time and Nana would be
busy. If it had been three or four months
ago, she could have helped with the baby
lambs – there was always lots to do at
lambing time – but the baby lambs were

big and healthy now, all weaned from their mums and grazing out on the lush grass in the far paddocks. She knew she could walk through the farmland down to the beach by following the creek and then taking the path that led down to a secluded sandy bay. But it wasn't much fun being on the beach on your own, even if there were seals swimming in the water and lying on the rocks further out at sea.

That was one of the only good things about being in Australia as far as Millie was concerned. She loved all animals, and there were so many interesting wild animals and birds to see here –

kangaroos, wide-eyed possums, spiny-backed echidna, cackling kookaburras and loud miner birds. There were even a couple of shy, gentle koalas who lived in a cluster of gum trees near the creek.

I guess Nana will probably want me to help with stuff on the farm this holiday, Millie thought, getting up. She pulled on some shorts and a T-shirt, rubbed sun cream into her face, arms and legs and pulled her wavy hair into a high ponytail.

Nana was in the large kitchen, the back door open on to the veranda, a fly screen stopping insects from coming in. She was sorting out some scraps of vegetables for the chickens. "Morning," she said cheerfully as Millie came in. "First day of the summer holidays. Bet that feels good?"

Millie forced a smile. "Yeah." She put some bread in the toaster.

"Once you've had your brekkie, we'll head out and feed the chooks," said Nana. "I thought you could look after them for me over the holidays. They need grain each day as well as scraps, the eggs need collecting and the chook house needs cleaning out. You'll give me a hand with all those things, won't you?"

"Sure," said Millie. Doing anything with animals was fun and she liked looking after the chickens. Nana had a number of different rare breeds of hens and they were all very pretty and tame.

"After we've done the chooks, Nancy, Nelly and the kids need feeding." Nancy and Nelly were goats. They'd both had babies – kids – a few months ago. "Then we'll head out in the ute and check on the sheep. This arvo we can start getting ready for Christmas."

"It sounds like there's a lot to do," said Millie, perking up.

Nana chuckled. "Your mum used to be glad to go back to school for a rest when the summer holidays ended!" She pointed to Millie's plate. "Eat up, kid. You're in for a busy day!"

Nana was right! She and Millie hardly
stopped all morning. Once the chickens
– or chooks as Nana called them – had
been fed and the eggs collected, they
turned the goats out in a small paddock
and cleaned out their pen. While they
were busy, one of the little black-
and-white kids – Pickle – escaped by
wriggling under the fence and Millie
had to catch him and carry him back. At
the same time Nana stopped his worried
mum, Nancy, from trying to knock the
fence down to get to him. Once Pickle
was safely back in his pen, they set off

in Nana's pick-up truck to check on the sheep. In the summer months, the sheep grazed on the pasture furthest away from the farmhouse. Akuna, Nana's friendly black-and-tan kelpie dog, sat in the back of the ute as they bounced along the dusty red tracks heading around the 250-hectare farm to check on the different flocks – or mobs as Nana called them.

Nana and Millie inspected the water troughs to make sure they were full and the fences to make sure they were all secure while Akuna rounded the sheep up, herding them into a large pen so that Nana and Millie could check that none of them were injured or ill. The air was filled with the sound of bleating as the sheep clustered together in the pen, squashing against each other before being let back out again. Millie had the job of holding the gate open and counting the sheep as they leapt through the narrow gap, one at a time, before trotting happily back out into the pasture.

Nana knew them all by name. "Don't

you be fooled when people tell you sheep are all the same," she told Millie. "They're just as individual as humans. My older ewes are like friends to me. I've had some of them eight or nine years."

Looking at the sheep milling around, Millie wasn't sure how Nana could tell them apart but she liked the idea of them having personalities.

"Do we need to feed them?" Millie asked.

"Not at this time of year," said Nana. "The grazing here's so good it could fatten a fencepost, but come late summer we might need to put feed out if the grass dries up."

By the time they had finished checking on the sheep, Nana and Millie were coated with a fine layer of red dust from the dry ground. The sun was high in the sky now and it was a relief to get back into the ute and feel the breeze against their hot faces.

"Now, before we eat lunch, I've got something to show you," said Nana. "I came to check on the barn yesterday and it seems we've had a guest move in." She stopped the ute outside the large barn that was used for sheep shearing. Nana kept merino sheep who had thick, woolly coats and most of the farm's income came from selling wool. Telling

Akuna to stay in the ute, she headed towards the barn.

Millie hopped out of the truck and followed her curiously. What was Nana going to show her?

The inside of the large barn had pens divided with partitions and a floor made of metal grating so that the sheep's droppings could fall to the earth below. Apart from at shearing time, the barn was usually empty. Nana put a finger to her lips and tiptoed across the metal floor. Millie followed her, breathing in the smell of sheep. Nana crouched down and pointed through the metal grating. Millie gasped. A creature with a fat,

grey-brown body and short legs was
right underneath her feet. As she stared,
he swivelled his head up and regarded
them warily. He had a fluffy, chubby-
cheeked face that looked a bit like a
koala's, small ears, a big black nose and
shining dark eyes. *A wombat!*

Wombats were shy creatures. Millie
had heard that some
farmers thought
wombats
were pests
because they
liked to dig
tunnels and
sometimes

caused damage to fences, but Nana was smiling fondly. "He must have discovered this place and thought it was wombat heaven," she whispered. "Plenty of soft soil and sheep poo to burrow in."

"He's gorgeous," Millie whispered back. Her eyes met her nana's and they both smiled.

"I thought you'd like to see him," said Nana, looking pleased. "Let's leave him be now though. Wombats don't like to be disturbed."

They tiptoed out of the barn.

"Poor old fella's going to be in for a shock when the shed fills up with sheep at shearing time," said Nana. "I think he might move out pretty hastily then but he can stay for now."

Millie sighed happily. "You have such amazing animals here in Australia."

Nana gave her a shrewd look. "Don't you mean *we* have amazing animals here in Australia," she corrected her. "This is your home too now, Millie."

Millie swallowed and looked down at the ground. Whatever Nana said, this wasn't really her home. She was always going to feel like she was just a visitor.

As they drove back to the farmhouse, Nana glanced across at her. "You remind me of your mum when she was eleven. Good with all the animals. Maybe you'll be a vet when you're older, like she was."

Millie shrugged, her throat tightening. She did want to be a vet, but she didn't want to talk about her mum. "Maybe," she muttered, looking out of the window.

She had a feeling Nana was waiting for her to say something more but she didn't want to and they drove in silence back to the farmhouse.

Chapter Three

That afternoon, they put up the
Christmas tree and decorated the house
and front door with a wreath and swags
made of Christmas bush that they cut
from the yard. Christmas bush was a
tree with small green leaves and cream-
coloured flowers that would turn a deep,

beautiful red at Christmas time.

"I'll also get some poinsettias in pots and put them around the house," Nana said as they started to decorate the Christmas tree. "They always make me feel festive. I guess you're more used to holly and pine though?"

Millie nodded. "It's weird, Christmas is the same in some ways," she said, as they hung the glass baubles and small stuffed animals on the tree. "But it's also really different." The decorations looked old and well-loved. Millie wondered if her mum had once hung them on the tree just like she was doing and tears suddenly prickled her eyes.

To distract herself, she asked Nana a question. "Will we have turkey for Christmas dinner?"

"Oh yes, some people have a barbie or eat seafood on Christmas Day but I like to have a traditional roast turkey and all the trimmings, followed by a pavlova," said Nana.

"Pavlova?" echoed Millie. "So not Christmas pudding then?"

"Your mum was never that fussed about Christmas pudding so when she was about five, we started having pavlova instead – meringue, whipped cream, fresh summer fruit. There's nothing to beat it, just you wait and see."

Millie felt a rush of unhappiness. Even though she didn't really like Christmas pudding that much either, she didn't want to have pavlova on Christmas Day. She wanted everything to be as it always was. She wanted Christmas in England with her mum. Millie turned abruptly away, blinking back her tears.

Nana fetched them both a glass of cold lemonade and brought in a plate of biscuits. "Now, when your mum was younger, I knitted her a giant Christmas stocking," she said. "I thought I might do the same for you." She picked up a box which held wool and knitting needles. "One thing about living on a sheep farm, you're never short of wool! Do you know how to knit?"

Millie shook her head.

"Well, sit yourself down and I'll teach you," said Nana.

Millie sat on the floor and tried to follow Nana's instructions but her mind kept wandering. All she could think about was how horrible it was going to be this Christmas without Mum. The knitting got all tangled up, despite Nana's instructions. "I can't do it!" she said, throwing the wool down in frustration. "It's impossible."

"There's no such thing as impossible," said Nana.

Millie jumped to her feet. "Yes, there is! It's impossible that Mum will ever come back!" she cried angrily.

Her nana's face softened. "Millie . . ."

But Millie had had enough of being nice and polite. She ran out of the lounge and into her bedroom. Flinging herself down on her bed, she sobbed. She heard the door opening and knew her nana was there.

"Oh, Millie," Nana said, coming over and stroking her back.

Millie didn't look round. She just sobbed harder. She knew Nana just wanted to comfort her, but nothing could make her feel better. Not ever.

On the night before Christmas Eve, a violent storm blew up. Rain lashed at the farmhouse and the wind howled as Millie, her dad and Nana ate supper around the wooden table.

"Will the sheep be OK?" Millie asked anxiously.

"Yes, there's plenty of shelter for them

from the trees," said Nana. "They're used to be being out in all weather." She glanced at the window. "It'll blow itself out by the morning."

Millie found it hard to get to sleep that night. She lay in bed listening to the storm raging, but she eventually dropped off and when she woke, all was quiet apart from the sound of Robert crowing. She went to the window. The cloudless early morning sky was a pale grey streaked with blue and the sun was just starting to rise. Tree branches littered the back yard, but the hen house had survived and in the distance, Millie could see the white shapes of sheep dotting the hillside. Everything looked calm and peaceful. It was as though the storm had never happened.

Millie got dressed and went to get some breakfast. Dad was off work now until January and he was already out in the yard, clearing up the branches. Nana was listening to the radio and looking worried as she bustled around the kitchen. "An oil tanker's capsized further up the coast," she said to Millie. "That's not good news for the local marine wildlife. Seals suffer badly when there's an oil spill. Maybe, once we've fed the chooks and the goats, we should head down to the bay and check the beach in case any seal pups have got stranded."

"OK," Millie said.

As soon as the animals were fed, they headed out in the ute and drove across the clifftops until they came to the secluded bay that curved round like a horseshoe. The top of the cliff was covered with springy grass and the sand on the beach below was golden. Waves broke into sprays of white foam as they hit the rocks around the headland. A steep, rocky path led down the cliff to the beach.

Millie bounded ahead of Nana, who was making her way carefully down the path. When she reached the bottom, the beach was totally empty, just dark boulders and stretches of pale sand covered with seaweed at the tide line.

Millie's eyes scanned the bay, looking for stranded seal pups, but to her relief she didn't see any. They were hopefully all safe with their mums out on the small rocky islands offshore. Suddenly, her eyes caught sight of something dark and small lying on the sand. At first glance she had thought it was just a rock, but now she noticed that it was moving.

She jogged towards it and as she got closer she stopped dead. It was a very small penguin with a blue-grey back and head and a creamy-white belly that was streaked with grey oil. Its large feet were a pale pink with dark tips and it had stubby little flippers that were flapping up and down. Opening its beak, it gave a sad cry.

"Oh, wow!" breathed Millie. She had only ever seen penguins in the zoo and on television before. She approached slowly, not wanting to scare it. She wondered if it would waddle into the

water and swim
away but it
didn't.
It looked lost
and confused
and, as Millie got
closer, she saw that
a lot of its feathers were coated with
sticky oil.

"Hey, there," she murmured. "It's OK,
I'm not going to hurt you."

The little penguin cried unhappily.
"Huk-huk!"

Millie's heart went out to the little
creature. It had clearly got caught
up in the oil slick and now it was

lost and alone. It probably missed its family as much as she missed her mum. Determination filled her. *I have to help it,* she thought.

Chapter Four

Millie slowly approached the penguin. "Don't worry," she murmured softly. "I'm going to help you."

To her relief, the penguin didn't try to escape. It stayed where it was on the sand, watching her with frightened silvery-grey eyes.

Millie wondered how to pick it up. She didn't want to get pecked by that long beak, and its feathers looked slippery from the oil. She untied her hoodie from round her waist and crouched down beside the penguin. Moving quickly, she wrapped the bird in her hoodie and scooped it up into her arms. Hopefully Nana would know what to do. They definitely couldn't leave it here on the beach where it might get eaten by hungry seals.

The penguin lay still in her arms.

Millie hurried to the base of the cliff where her grandmother was reaching the end of the path. "Nana! Look! A

penguin! It was on the beach." Millie
pulled the hoodie back a little to show
what she was holding.

"It must have got caught in the oil
spill," said Nana. "Poor thing. It doesn't
look too good." She gently stroked the
top of the penguin's head with one
finger. It gave a piercing cry. "It's a girl,"

said Nana. "You can tell from the beak. The females have thinner beaks and smaller heads than the males."

"She's so small – she must only be a baby," said Millie.

Nana smiled. "I think she *is* young. But because of her feathers, not because of her size. She's a Fairy Penguin, or as most people call them these days – a Little Penguin. They're the smallest of all the penguins."

"How do you know so much about penguins?" Millie asked her grandmother, impressed.

"Your mum was penguin-mad when she was growing up. Her bedroom walls were covered in penguin pictures. She volunteered at the penguin sanctuary as soon as she was old enough."

"What should we do?" asked Millie anxiously.

"Let's take her home and phone the sanctuary," said Nana. "She won't be able to survive with oil on her feathers. If penguins try and preen the oil off they get ill. And even if they don't do that, the oil mats their feathers together so they get cold and they can't swim as easily. The sanctuary will be able to clean her up and if she survives, they'll release her back into the wild."

Millie carried the precious bundle

carefully up the cliff and got into the pick-up truck. The penguin nestled against her chest. She gazed down at her as Nana drove back to the farmhouse. The penguin stared up at her, its tiny eyes dazed and shocked.

When they got back to the house, Akuna came bounding out to greet them. The penguin stiffened and struggled in Millie's arms, making a panicked yelping sound a bit like a puppy.

"No, Akuna," said Millie quickly. "Don't frighten her."

"Akuna, down," said Nana. The dog backed off obediently and lay down.

They went inside and Nana phoned the sanctuary. Millie cuddled the penguin and listened to Nana's side of the conversation.

"I see. That must be making it hard for you, Kathleen. OK, well, what should we do?" Nana said. "Yes, I'm sure we can manage that. And you'll email the pattern over to me? Great, I'll get one knitted in no time. Hopefully the road will be passable soon and we'll bring her in then." Nana clicked the phone off.

"What did they say?" Millie demanded.

"The sanctuary is on an island and the road across to it is flooded," said

Nana, frowning. "We can't get there today. Kathleen, the sanctuary's director, knows me because I've brought them the occasional stranded penguin before and she worked there when your mum used to help out. She said she's happy for us to look after this little one here until the road's clear. So, are you prepared to be a penguin caretaker for a few days?"

"Oh yes!" breathed Millie in delight. The penguin was a warm bundle in her arms and she desperately wanted to help it. "What do we need to do? Should we wash the oil off her feathers?"

"Not straight away," said Nana. "Kathleen is sending me some instructions for how to do that, but she said that penguins often find being bathed very stressful so we need to let this one build up her strength for twenty-four hours before we try. In the meantime, it looks like I have some knitting to do!"

"Knitting?" echoed Millie in surprise.

Nana nodded. "To stop penguins preening themselves and swallowing the oil, the sanctuary put jumpers on them. They're emailing me a pattern so I can knit one to keep this little lady warm and stop her preening."

Just then, the back door opened and Dad walked in.

"Dad! Look!" Millie said, showing him the penguin in her arms.

"A penguin!" he exclaimed in astonishment. Millie quickly explained what had happened while Nana got her knitting things out. Dad's eyes went a bit misty as he looked at the penguin in Millie's arms. "Your mum always had a soft spot for penguins. On the top of our wedding cake, we had a penguin bride and groom. Do you remember?" he said to Nana.

"Oh yes," she said, nodding.

Dad cleared his throat and blinked. "Well, I'd better go into town and get this one some fish."

"Pilchards and anchovies," Nana put in.

Dad smiled. "This is not what I was expecting to be doing on Christmas Eve, that's for sure! Are you going to think of a name for her?" he said to Millie.

"Maybe best not to," said Nana quickly. "We don't want to get too attached. She's not looking well and she may not survive. Even if she does, she'll be off to the sanctuary soon."

Millie knew it was too late for her not to feel attached to the little penguin. "The sheep have names and they're not pets," she pointed out to Nana. "I'll think of a name. We can't just keep calling her the penguin." She thought for a moment. "I know. How about Evie? Because we found her on Christmas Eve."

"Perfect," said Dad. He gently stroked Evie's head. "Right, Evie, we'd better get you some food."

He grabbed the car keys and set off. Millie fetched a bowl of water and offered Evie a drink. She took a few mouthfuls but then flopped back against Millie's chest. Millie bit her lip as she remembered what Nana had said about Evie not being very well. *Please be OK,* she thought. *Please survive.*

Nana's knitting needles clacked together as she started to make a

brightly-coloured jumper. Evie drifted off
to sleep. As her eyes closed, Millie placed
her carefully on the couch, surrounded
by cushions so she couldn't fall off. She
edged closer to her nana, remembering
what Nana had said about needing to
knit a jumper for Evie.

"Can I help?" she asked. "I want to
make her a jumper too."

Nana looked surprised but then she
nodded. "Sure." She found Millie two
knitting needles and some green wool
and showed her how to wind the wool
on to the needles and move the needles
together to make a row of knitting. They
sat, side by side, knitting together. Nana

was three times as fast as Millie! Millie
kept dropping stitches and losing count
but this time she kept going. She really
wanted to help Evie.

"Do you think Evie's missing her
mum?" she asked.

"Well, penguins leave their parents
once they get their adult feathers and are
old enough to swim," explained Nana.
"But she'll be missing her friends, for
sure. Fairy penguins live in colonies on
the islands off the coast. The sanctuary is
near to one of the largest colonies."

"Do they just look after penguins at
the sanctuary?" Millie asked.

"No, they take in any wild animals

that are found injured or lost. They always have albatross and shearwaters in, as well as some mammals like possums, wallabies and echidnas. Kathleen who runs it is great. You'll like her. She was an assistant when your mum used to volunteer."

Millie hesitated, torn between not wanting to talk about her mum but also being fascinated to know more about the sanctuary. "What did Mum do when she was there?"

"All the dirty work!" said Nana with a smile. "Cleaning out cages and tanks, but she didn't care. She was just happy to be near the animals and birds. They used to let her watch operations when she got older – I think it was one of the reasons she was so determined to become a vet. After she'd been helping there a few years, she was allowed to assist with the rehabilitation of the penguins and give tours to the visitors." Nana shot her a look. "She always gave the penguins names. You're a lot like her, Millie. You really are."

Millie felt a hard lump form in her throat but she swallowed it. For once hearing about her mum wasn't making her feel upset; she liked hearing she was similar to her. It was so strange to think of Mum having a whole life before she had Millie though – before she moved to the UK and became a mum.

"Why did she like penguins so much?" she asked.

"They made her laugh. She said they were really funny. You might think that because they live in such big groups and look alike there wouldn't be much difference between them, but your mum always said they had completely different personalities."

"Like sheep," said Millie, remembering what Nana had told her at the start of the holidays.

Nana nodded.

"I want to work with animals when

I'm older," said Millie. She took a breath and met Nana's eyes. "Like Mum."

Nana smiled. "Good on you, kid."

They continued to knit in silence. Eventually, they had two jumpers. Nana did the hard bits of making holes for Evie's flippers and head and finishing the hems off. "All done!" she said, at last. "Now, we just need to get one on her."

Evie cawed a few times but didn't struggle as they gently put the striped jumper over her head and eased her flippers through the armholes. They placed her in a large metal dog crate covered with a blanket so that it would be dark like the burrow she would usually sleep in. When Dad came back, they offered Evie some of the fish he had bought. But Evie didn't want it. She just sat, huddled in her jumper, her head drooping, at the back of the crate.

"She doesn't look very happy," Millie said to Nana. "Why isn't she eating?"

Nana put a hand on her shoulder. "She's probably in shock. Try again in twenty minutes."

But twenty minutes later, Evie still refused the fish. Dad had gone out to repair the fences and Nana was making

the early preparations for Christmas
dinner the next day. Millie helped by
setting the table in the dining room but
she kept coming back into the kitchen
and shooting anxious glances at Evie.
"Why don't you get her out of the crate
and give her a cuddle?" said Nana. "She
may be feeling lonely. Penguins are used
to being very close to other penguins."

Millie opened the crate door. Evie
lifted her head and cawed plaintively.
"Come on, Evie," encouraged Millie. "I'll
take you out."

Evie waddled slowly towards her and
stopped by the door, her eyes looking
trustingly up at Millie. Millie scooped

her up and took her to the couch. She
put the TV on and they watched a
Christmas carol concert. Evie nestled
into Millie's arms. She seemed happier
now she was out of the crate.

Nana brought over some fish in a
bowl. Millie wrinkled her nose at the
smell but picked a piece up and held it in
front of Evie's nose, waving it temptingly.

"Yummy fish, Evie! Mmm!" she said.

To her delight, Evie's beak opened. Millie dropped the fish in and with a few clacks of her beak, Evie swallowed it.

For the rest of the day and evening, Millie stayed with Evie, offering her fish and water. She talked to her, sang carols and cuddled her close. At bedtime, Evie seemed happy to go into her crate and settle down. She had a drink of water then tucked her beak under her flipper, her eyes half-closing.

"Night, Evie," whispered Millie, shutting the crate door. "I'll see you in the morning."

Her dad got up from the armchair and came over. "Time for you to leave some

treats out for Santa," he said. "Nana
says your mum used to leave him some
biscuits and a bottle of beer – as well as
a carrot or two for his reindeer."

Millie fetched everything from the
kitchen and laid it out by the fireplace
where Nana had hung the stocking
she'd knitted for her. "One last Christmas
wish," said Dad, putting his arm across
her shoulders. They'd always had a

tradition of making wishes together on Christmas Eve.

"I don't have one," Millie said but then she glanced at Evie, sleeping in her crate, and changed her mind. "Actually, I do." She pressed her lips together and made the wish silently in her head: *Santa, please make Evie well again.*

Chapter Five

The moment Millie opened her eyes the next morning, her first thought was of Evie. Had the little penguin made it through the night?

Leaping out of bed, she raced to the kitchen, her heart pounding. *Oh, please, please, please be OK*, she pleaded.

As she passed the open lounge door, she saw that the giant stocking Nana had knitted was now lumpy with presents from Santa but Millie didn't stop. She raced into the kitchen and threw herself on the floor beside the crate, lifting the blanket up.

"*Brrrr-EEEEE!*" Evie waddled towards her, making a strange cry. It started off a bit like a donkey braying but then it rose into a high squeal. Her beak opened again. "*Brrrr-EEEEE!*" she repeated impatiently.

Millie felt a huge rush of relief. "Evie! You're still alive!" And not just alive, she realised in delight, but looking much brighter. The penguin's silvery-grey eyes had lost the dazed look they'd had the day before and she seemed far more alert. She cried again.

"Are you hungry?" Millie hurried to the fridge and got the plastic box of fish out. She opened the lid.

When she turned round, she saw that Evie had hopped out of the crate. Smelling the fish, she waddled over to Millie, her flippers flapping excitedly. Millie grinned and pulled a fish out of the box. Evie's beak opened eagerly and she gobbled it up. Millie fed her three more fish.

"Hey, she's looking better this

morning." Millie turned round to see Nana in the doorway.

"She is, isn't she?" she said, her eyes shining.

"And Santa seems to have called by," said Nana, nodding back towards the lounge. "Are you going to open your pressies?"

"Later," said Millie. Right now, all she could think about was Evie. "Can we wash Evie, Nana? We need to get rid of all the oil on her feathers."

"Okey-doke, but first we'd better feed the chooks and goats," said Nana. "The animals don't know it's Christmas Day. They'll be hungry and wanting their brekkie."

"Don't worry, I'll see to them," said Dad, coming in and heading for the back door. "Then I'll start making Christmas lunch while you two get on with Operation Penguin Clean-Up! Happy Christmas, Millie!"

"Happy Christmas, Dad!" Millie beamed. She felt like a weight had lifted off her shoulders.

Nana made Millie eat some toast and then she prepared the kitchen for penguin bath time. She kitted herself and Millie out with waterproof aprons, spread a plastic sheet over the kitchen table, fetched some old nail brushes and toothbrushes, then filled a large basin with warm water, along with a little dishwashing detergent. While Millie held Evie in her arms, Nana tested the temperature of the water with a thermometer.

"It needs to be forty-one degrees," she said, checking the instructions Kathleen from the sanctuary had emailed over. "As close as possible to Evie's body temperature. Yep, that's the ticket! Let's get her jumper off and get her in."

Millie put Evie down on the table. As
she took off her jumper, the little penguin
waddled over to the bowl of water and
flapped her flippers. "I think she *wants*
to go in," said Millie. She picked the
penguin up and gently lifted her into
the warm, soapy water. Evie flapped her

flippers a few times and then stood still as Nana began to gently scrub at her feathers with a toothbrush. The water soon turned a murky grey.

"Time for a refill," said Nana.

It took them two hours and five basins of soapy water, but at last all the oil seemed to be off Evie's feathers. There was a white patch on the tip of her right flipper that had been covered up by the oil. They rinsed her with several basins of fresh, clean water and then Nana got out a heat lamp she used when she was caring for orphaned or sick lambs. "We'll dry her with this then put the clean jumper on her."

"Does she still need to wear a jumper now that she's clean?" said Millie.

"We've done a pretty good job but there may be a tiny bit of oil left on her feathers and we don't want her eating it," said Nana. "Even a small amount could poison her. It'll be safer for her to wear a jumper until one of the vets at the sanctuary can check her over properly. I'll give them a ring tomorrow and see if the road is open."

Millie stayed with Evie, keeping her still under the heat lamp and feeding her fish, while Nana helped Dad finish off the preparations for Christmas lunch. The turkey had gone into the oven first thing, filling the kitchen with the delicious smell of roasting meat. The potatoes, parsnips and carrots had all been peeled. When Evie was dry and dressed in a jumper again, Dad suggested they should open their presents.

Millie carried Evie through to the lounge and the little penguin waddled around the rug, exploring. Spotting a loose thread, she started to tug at it with her beak. "No, Evie!" said Millie, gently moving her away from it. Evie gave her a cheeky look and waddled straight back over.

"I can see we'd better watch this one," said Nana with a grin.

"She's definitely looking perkier today," said Dad.

"Huk-huk!" said Evie as if she agreed.

Millie carried her away from the loose thread again and sat down with her stocking as well as other presents from Nana, Dad and from friends back at home. As Millie started to unwrap the presents, Evie had a great time tossing wrapping paper around her with her beak. Santa had brought Millie lip balms in different flavours, marker pens, hair scrunchies, books and some cute little china ornaments shaped like animals. Her friend Lola had sent her a giant box of her favourite sweets and Dad had bought her a subscription to a wildlife magazine. Nana gave her a towelling beach hoodie, a bright blue swimsuit and a matching beach towel.

"I thought you could use them tomorrow at the barbie on the beach," she said. "Do you like them?"

"Oh yes. Thanks, Nana!" Millie felt awkward. She had been dreading Christmas so much and not wanting to think about it, that she hadn't got Nana a present. Now, she felt terrible. Nana had been so brilliant with Evie. "I'm . . . I'm really sorry I haven't got you anything."

"No worries," said Nana. "Having you

and your dad living here with me is all I want. Least this year I won't be doing the washing up on my own!" Her eyes twinkled and she stood up. "Now, I'd better get started on that pavlova."

Her words gave Millie an idea. "Could . . . could I help you make it?" She glanced at Evie who had settled down in a nest she'd made of wrapping paper and was tucking her beak under her flipper, ready for a nap. "I think Evie will be fine for a while on her own."

Nana beamed. "That would be the best Christmas gift ever, kid. Let's get baking!"

The Christmas lunch was delicious.

The turkey, roast vegetables and gravy were cooked just the way Millie liked them. Afterwards, while Evie waddled around the table legs, she tucked into the gooey pavlova, thick whipped cream bursting over light, crisp meringue and plump red raspberries.

"So?" Nana said. "What do you think of pavlova?"

"It's yummy!" said Millie. "In fact," she smiled as she allowed herself to admit the truth,

"I think it's much nicer than Christmas pudding!"

Nana held up her hand and high-fived her. "We'll make an Aussie of you yet, kid!"

Millie caught her dad's smile. She'd been sure she was going to feel like crying all day, but actually the hours had flown by with looking after Evie, opening the presents and getting dinner ready.

Evie stopped beside her chair and opened her beak. "*Brrr-EEEE*?" she said hopefully.

Millie grinned. "You want some more fish, Evie? Come on then, let's get you some." She scooped up the little penguin and carried her through to the kitchen, a warm feeling tingling through her as Evie cuddled against her chest.

Chapter Six

The next day, Evie was looking even brighter. She followed Millie around the house like a little shadow. Wherever Millie went, Evie did too. Nana rang the sanctuary and spoke to Kathleen.

"The road to the sanctuary's open again now," she told Millie when she got off the phone. "But they've got so many penguins to deal with after the oil spill, they've asked if we can hang on to Evie for another day or two." She smiled. "I said I thought that would be OK with you."

"More than OK!" said Millie in delight. Evie would have to go to the sanctuary at some point so she could be released back into the wild, but Millie wanted as long as possible with her. "I won't go to the beach," she said. "I'd better stay home and look after her."

"No, no," said Nana. "You'll only be out for a few hours and I can keep an eye on Evie. It'll do you good to go to the beach and have a swim with the kids from school. Make sure you take your boogie board and cozzie."

"OK," said Millie, sighing. She didn't really feel like going; she'd much rather stay with Evie. She knew she'd probably end up just hanging round with her dad because everyone from school would be with their friends, but Nana seemed keen for her to go.

Later in the morning, she and Dad set off. The barbie was happening on the main beach in town. It was a bright sunny day but there was a gentle breeze which stopped it feeling too hot. There were so many people out on the beach.

It seemed like the whole town was there! Steak, sausages and seafood were being grilled on barbecues and people had laid out bread and tubs of salad behind wind breakers. Children were splashing in the shallows and playing with boogie boards, while the grown-ups sat around on beach chairs, laughing and talking. There were lots of games of cricket and volleyball going on, too.

Millie and her dad had to walk quite far along the beach to find a patch of sand where they could lay out their things. As they spread out their towels, there was a cry of "Heads!" and they ducked as a cricket ball landed with a thud on the sand beside them.

"Sorry about that, mate!" said a man, jogging over.

"No worries,' said Dad, picking up the ball and throwing it back to him.

"Do you want to join in?" said the man, nodding towards the game.

Dad glanced at Millie.

"Go on," she said with a grin. She knew he loved cricket. "I'm going to paddle in the water."

Dad grinned back and went to join in with the cricket game.

Millie ambled down to the sea. The sand was warm and she was glad she had kept her flip flops on. When she

reached the damp sand, she kicked them off and let her toes sink into it. The waves lapped over her feet. She looked around at everyone playing games, swimming, talking to friends and for a moment she felt lonely. It would be nice to have someone to hang round with. She paddled in the water for a bit then moved to the dry sand. Sitting down, she started to make a sand sculpture of a penguin.

"Hey, that's really good!"

Millie looked up and saw Alice from school standing there, a boogie board in one hand. "Hi," she said with a shy smile. She suddenly remembered something.

"Has your dog had her puppies yet?"

"Not yet," said Alice. "Any day now. I hope it all goes OK."

Millie saw worry flash across her classmate's eyes. "I'm sure it will. I bet they'll be super-cute."

"Puppies always are." Alice grinned and looked at the sculpture. "Is that a penguin?"

Millie nodded. "I'm looking after one at the moment."

"How come?" said Alice curiously.

Millie explained about Evie. "That's so cool," said Alice, dropping her boogie board and kneeling down beside her on the sand. "I'd love to look after a penguin. You're really lucky."

"I'm just glad she's all right," said
Millie. "I was really worried about her
before we got the oil off."

"How did you do that?" asked Alice.

Millie told her about giving Evie a
bath. Alice seemed genuinely interested.
When Millie told her about the special

jumper Evie wore, Alice gasped. "Oh, wow! I love knitting. Maybe I could make a penguin jumper."

"Yeah, if you want to," said Millie. "There are lots of other penguins at the sanctuary who got caught in the oil spill. They need jumpers too. You could come round and get the pattern off my nana."

"I'd really like that!" said Alice. "Maybe I could meet Evie too?"

"You'll have to come soon then,' said Millie. "She'll have to go to the sanctuary in a few days."

"Tomorrow?" suggested Alice. "I can ask Mum to drive me over."

"Great," said Millie happily. "I can

show you the other animals at the farm.
There are the goats and sheep and
Akuna, Nana's dog . . ."

They chatted about animals for a bit
longer and Alice helped Millie finish the
sculpture off. Then a woman with long
plaited hair came over to them. "Alice,
the food's going to be ready soon."

"OK. Mum, this is Millie," said Alice.
"She's a friend from school. She just
moved here a few months ago from
England."

Millie felt a rush of warmth – Alice
had described her as a friend!

"Hi, Millie. I'm Jo. So this is your first
Aussie Christmas?" said Alice's mum.

"What do you think of having a barbie on the beach on Boxing Day?"

"It's fun," said Millie. She glanced towards her and Dad's things. "Though I'm not sure we'll actually get round to having a barbie. Dad hasn't even lit ours yet. He's been too busy playing cricket."

"I'll tell him to come and share ours," said Jo easily. "We've got heaps more food than we can eat." She headed over to have a chat with the group of cricketers.

"Is your dad playing cricket?" Millie asked Alice.

"No, my brothers and uncles are, but Dad's a fire fighter. He was called out to fight a bush fire yesterday," said Alice.

Millie heard the sad note in her voice. "It must have been hard not having him with you on Christmas Day."

"Yeah, but at least he'll be home soon." Alice's eyes met Millie's. She didn't say anything about Millie's mum, but Millie saw the sympathy in her gaze and it was enough. The warm feeling that had surged through her when Alice called her a friend increased. "Hey, should we go in the water before we eat?" she said.

"Yeah!" said Alice.

Millie ran to get her boogie board and they splashed into the sea together. Alice showed Millie how to lie on her tummy

on the board and ride the waves in.
Finally, shaking water out of their hair,
they ran up the beach to the barbie. Dad
was already there, tucking into a plate of
steak and salad.

"Having fun?" he asked Millie.

She beamed. "Oh, yes!" she replied.

Chapter Seven

Alice's mum dropped her at the farm the next day and Nana offered to take her home later. When Alice saw Evie, her face lit up. "She is so cute!"

Evie waddled over to Alice and gave her a stare, as if weighing her up.

Alice crouched down. "Hello, there,

Evie. I've heard all about you."

The penguin flapped her flippers as if she approved. Millie hid her smile. Last night, she'd told Evie all about Alice too!

The little penguin let Alice tickle her under her chin, rubbing the side of her head against Alice's hand.

"I love her jumper," Alice said.

"Nana's printed you off a copy of the pattern," said Millie. "We can do some knitting later."

But first they played with Evie and fed her. Then while the penguin had a rest, Millie showed Alice around the farm, introducing her to Akuna, the goats, the sheep and the wombat who was still

living under the shearing shed. Millie
had named him Walter.

"I wish I lived on a farm like this one,"
said Alice as they went back into the
house. "You're really lucky, Millie."

Nana was in the kitchen and
overheard.

"Feel free to come over any time,
there are always jobs that need doing."
She fetched them some lemonade and
cookies. "Now, I rang the penguin
sanctuary while you were out, Millie.
They've said they can take Evie in
today."

"Today?" echoed Millie, her heart
sinking. She bent down and picked up

the little penguin, who had waddled
eagerly over to meet her.

Nana nodded. "It's for the best, kid.
She's not a pet and the longer Evie stays
with us the harder it will be for her to
survive in the wild. You want her to be
set free, don't you?"

Millie swallowed as she looked at Evie,
snuggling into her arms. "Yes," she said,
sighing.

"We could take her over later this arvo
after Alice goes home," said Nana. "Or I
could call Alice's mum and see if it's OK
for her to come with us to the sanctuary
and we could all go after lunch. If you'd
like to come with us, Alice?"

"I'd love to!" said Alice, giving Millie a hopeful look.

"OK," said Millie, trying to be brave. She dropped a kiss on the top of Evie's head. She couldn't bear the thought of saying goodbye to her, but she didn't want Alice to think she was a baby so she forced the tears back.

For the rest of the morning, the two girls played with Evie. They also tried to knit, but Evie kept pecking at the wool and getting tangled up in it.

"I'll take the pattern home and knit a jumper there," said Alice. "I think a superhero jumper with a cape would look really cute – or maybe a pink one

with little fairy wings."

"They'd look adorable but they'd be
no good for the penguins," said Millie.
"The sanctuary told Nana the jumpers
had to be completely plain with nothing
for the penguins to get tangled up on."

"I've got a cuddly toy penguin at

home, I might make one for him!" said Alice. "But I'll make a proper one to send to the sanctuary as well."

The time flew by and all too soon, the girls were getting into Nana's ute with Evie. Millie cuddled her the whole way to the sanctuary. She could hardly believe the time had come to say goodbye. *I don't want to,* she thought. But looking down at the little penguin nestled in her arms, she knew she couldn't keep her. She had to do what was best for Evie.

She felt Alice give her a gentle nudge. "You're doing the right thing," she said softly as Millie glanced over at her.

Millie nodded and forced a smile.

Kathleen, the sanctuary's director, was
a bit younger than Nana, with brown
hair streaked with grey. She greeted
them warmly and showed them through
to one of the examination rooms where
she introduced them to Amy, a young
vet. Amy removed Evie's jumper and
examined her, checking her feathers,
lifting her flippers, opening her beak
and listening to her heartbeat with a
stethoscope.

"You sure can tell whose daughter
she is," said Kathleen, smiling as Millie

soothed Evie and held her firmly but
gently, even when the penguin struggled
slightly, objecting to the vet opening
her beak.

"Yep, she's a chip off the old block, no
doubt about it," said Nana proudly.

"I met your mum when she was just a
few years older than you," Kathleen said
to Millie. "You remind me of her."

Millie felt a rush of happiness.

"Well, this little lady's in excellent condition," said Amy, finishing her examination and stroking Evie's head. "You've done a great job looking after her. She just needs to build up the natural water-proofing of her feathers then she'll be able to go back into the wild. We've got a large group of birds in at the moment so she'll have plenty of friends to get to know."

"Do you want to come with us and watch her join the rest of the group?" said Kathleen. "Or, if you'd rather, you can say goodbye to her here."

"No, I want to see her join the other

penguins," said Millie quickly.

They said goodbye to Amy, then Kathleen took them through to a large outdoor enclosure. There was a pool in the centre surrounded by sandy earth and wooden nesting boxes half-hidden by long, dry grass.

"There are heaps of penguins!" exclaimed Alice.

Some were swimming in the water or resting in the mouths of burrows, while others were waddling round the water's edge, waggling their flippers and cawing to each other. Evie stiffened in Millie's arms as they reached the entrance. She made an uncertain yelping sound.

"You really have got your hands full," Nana said to Kathleen.

"Tell me about it," said Kathleen. "This oil spill has completely overstretched us. So many penguins needed our help. We've been struggling to find the money to make sure they all have the care they need. It's completely drained our resources. I'm going to have to organise some fundraising events but right now, I'm too busy to plan anything." She looked worried. "I hope we manage to get through the next few months. Now," she turned to Millie, "are you ready to take Evie inside?"

Millie nodded, her throat tight. Evie was pressing close to her chest. She didn't seem very sure about joining the big group of penguins.

Kathleen unlocked the gate and while Nana and Alice waited outside, she went into the enclosure with Millie and Evie. Millie knelt down and Evie looked up at her uncertainly.

"It's OK, Evie. This is going to be

your new home for a little while," Millie
whispered. "You're going to make lots
of new friends and then you'll get to go
back out to the sea with them. You'll like
that, I promise."

Evie peered at the other penguins.
Millie gently lifted her up and set her
down on the ground, closer to them. Evie
didn't move. Millie took a deep breath.
This was so hard . . .

Another penguin noticed Evie. It waddled closer, giving her a curious look. Putting its head on one side, it made a *huk-huk* sound.

Evie looked away.

The other penguin waddled round her until it could see her face and then gave another *huk-huk,* louder this time.

Evie swung her head round to the other side, but Millie saw her take a sneaky peek back at the other penguin. It waddled all the way round her again and came closer, bending its head down and peering up into her face.

"*Brrr-EEEE?*"

Evie hesitated and then opened her

beak. "*Brrr-EEEE*," she replied.

The penguin swayed from side to side, looking excited. It flapped its flippers.

Evie took a few steps towards it. She bobbed her head up and down and it copied her. They started waddling round each other in delight.

"Looks like Evie's made a friend," said Kathleen softly, smiling at Millie. "And I bet it's the first of many."

The two penguins waddled off towards the water, side by side, their flippers almost touching.

Millie felt a wild rush of emotions – sadness that this was the moment Evie was going to join the other penguins,

but also joy. Evie was healthy, she was happy, and she was going to be OK.

"You can come back and visit her whenever you like," said Kathleen as Millie straightened up. "In fact, when you're twelve, you could come and help out here. If we're still open, of course."

"You have to stay open," said Millie, thinking of all the animals and birds who needed help. "The sanctuary can't shut."

"I hope you're right," said Kathleen with a sigh, leading the way out of the enclosure.

As she shut the gate behind them, Alice gave Millie a smile and Nana pulled her into an unexpected hug. "You did the right thing, kiddo," she said, her voice gruff.

Millie looked back and saw Evie diving into the water with her new friend. "I know," she said.

Chapter Eight

That night, Millie's dreams were filled with little penguins wearing jumpers. They were waddling round, knitting jumpers themselves and getting all tangled up in the wool. When Millie woke up, a plan burst into her brain. *I know how we can help the sanctuary!* she thought, sitting bolt upright in bed. She ran downstairs to tell Nana her idea.

"A New Year's Eve knit-a-thon?" said Nana, her eyebrows rising into her grey hair. "To raise money for the sanctuary?"

"Yes, we could get everyone to come here and they could knit jumpers and other things. We could sell them and give the money to the sanctuary!" Millie's eyes shone. "What do you think? Would people do it?"

Nana's face slowly creased into a smile. "I reckon they would!" she said. "I'll donate the wool and we can bake some cakes and cookies for the knitting session and then turn it into a proper New Year's

Eve party. All people need to do is turn up and knit – and have fun!"

"Alice loves to knit. I bet she'll come if she's free," said Millie. "I'll ask her."

She and Alice had swapped numbers the day before. Millie grabbed her mobile phone and called her friend.

"Yeah, count me in!" said Alice after Millie had quickly explained her idea. "I can get some other kids from school to come along too, if that's

OK? We used to have a knitting club last year. Do you want me to ask them?"

"Yes, please!" said Millie. "The more the merrier!"

"Cool, I'll get in touch with everyone," said Alice. "Leave it to me. But I'd better go now – Sasha's just started having her pups!"

"Oh my goodness, I hope everything goes well," said Millie. "Let me know!"

"I will!" promised Alice.

Millie had been dreading her first day without Evie to look after, but there was so much to do and organise that she hardly had time to feel sad. Nana got in contact with her friends and then she and Millie downloaded some patterns from the internet and sorted a load of wool out. There were all the usual farm chores to do, as well.

Millie phoned Kathleen and told her what they were planning. She was delighted and promised to come along and join in. "Evie's settled in very well," she told Millie. "I'll send you some pictures if you like."

After the call ended, Kathleen emailed the photos over.

"There she is," said Millie, spotting the white mark on her flipper. The pictures showed Evie swimming with the other penguins, waddling round with them and resting in a nesting box. She looked very happy to be with other penguins again.

"Evie's been making friends then?" said Nana, looking over Millie's shoulder at the photos on the computer screen.

Millie's mobile phone buzzed. She checked it and saw that Alice had sent her a photo of Sasha with five tiny black pups snuggled up beside her.

Can't wait for you to meet them! Alice had written, followed by lots of smiley faces.

Millie sent her back a thumbs up and a clapping hands emoji.

Nana chuckled. "Seems to me Evie's

not the only one making friends!"

Millie grinned.

The knit-a-thon was an even bigger success than Millie had imagined. Loads of people turned up – old and young – and by the end of the afternoon there were piles of teddy jumpers, knitted toys, baby blankets and colourful scarves all made from the gorgeous, soft wool from Nana's sheep. The people who couldn't knit bought the items and the cash box quickly filled up.

Kathleen was delighted. "Everyone's been so generous!" she said. "It's going to

make a real difference to the sanctuary."
She hugged Millie. "Thank you so much
for organising this!"

"Three cheers for Millie!" Alice called,
jumping to her feet. "Hip, hip . . ."

"HOORAY!" everyone shouted.

The girls and boys from school who
had come along surrounded Millie, their
cheers getting louder with each hooray.
Millie glowed. For the first time since
she'd moved to Australia, she felt like she
really belonged and it was all thanks to
Evie and the penguin sanctuary.

Dad turned the music on. "Let's get this
party started!" he shouted.

As the sun sank in the sky, everyone

danced and ate. Nana had made an enormous pot of three-bean chilli that she put out for people to help themselves to. There were mounds of nachos, dips and garlic bread and other people had brought salads and desserts. Everyone dug in to the delicious food.

"This is so much fun!" said Millie as she and Alice finished eating and began dancing again.

"We've got to stay up till midnight!" Alice said, grabbing her hands and swinging her

round. "I've never stayed up on New Year's Eve before."

"Me neither," said Millie.

They danced until midnight, stopping only to get drinks and ice creams. As the final seconds of the old year ticked by, Nana put on the radio and everyone gathered outside and counted down together along with the radio.

"Ten . . . nine . . . eight . . . seven . . . six . . . five . . . four . . . three . . . two . . . one . . . HAPPY NEW YEAR!"

Dad grabbed Millie and Nana and pulled them into a bear hug. "Happy new year!" he said, squeezing them both tightly.

"Happy new year," said Nana, her face kind and smiling.

Millie stared up at the full moon overhead and felt hope well up inside her. It had been a horrible year, the worst of her life, but it was over now. She still missed her mum every day and she always would, but it hurt a bit less than it had. Finally, Australia was starting to feel like home.

She clicked the home button of her phone and her lock screen flashed on. It was a photo of Evie, dressed in her little stripey jumper, her head on one side as she stared straight at the camera. Millie gently touched the screen. Everything had changed when Evie had come into her life. Millie was sure the little penguin would soon forget her, but she would never forget Evie. Even if she lived to be a hundred.

Thank you, Evie, she thought, touching the photo with her finger.

"Millie! Are you ready to dance some

more?" Alice skipped over from where she had been wishing her mum and dad and two brothers a happy new year.

"Deffo!" said Millie with a smile.

One year later...

Millie stood on the beach of the island where the sanctuary was. She'd been volunteering there ever since she turned twelve in July. Like her mum, she mainly got to do all the dirty jobs but she didn't care. She just loved being around the animals. Kathleen had said that when she was older she'd be able to help more with rehabilitation and watch the vets at work.

One of her favourite things to do was to watch the penguin parade at sunset. It was when all the penguins came back from the sea, waddled up the beach in a big group and headed into their burrows for the night.

Millie sat on the sand at the base of the sand dune near a wooden nesting box. Would she come? Yes. There she was! A little penguin with a white tip on her right wing came waddling determinedly up the beach with a small group of other penguins. As they all headed into their own burrows, Evie made her way over to Millie and looked up at her with her silvery-grey eyes.

"*Brrrrr-EEEEE?*"

Millie grinned and made the same
sound back.

"*Brrrr-EEEEE,*" said Evie, as if agreeing. She dipped her head and pulled at Millie's trainer laces with her beak.

"Oh no, you don't," said Millie, pulling her feet away quickly. Nana would be cross if Evie wrecked one more pair of her shoe laces!

Evie flapped her flippers and waddled into her burrow.

"Good night, Evie," Millie whispered.

Evie stuck her head out of the hole and for a moment, her bright eyes met Millie's. She bobbed her head up and down then she disappeared back inside. Millie smiled to herself and then set off across the sand dunes as the sun sank down into the horizon, its rays painting pink and crimson streaks across the evening sky.

The End

Love animals? Here's another
great story by Tilda Kelly!

Chapter One

Ruby Turner turned the pages of her animal encyclopaedia. As her eyes ran over the pages on marsupials, she recited the facts in her head. *Red kangaroo weight: 150kg; hairy-nosed wombat weight: 40kg . . .*

When Ruby was older, she was going to be a vet and work at Green Gates

Wildlife Sanctuary where her mum had

a job as a nurse. She

pushed her chin-

length, brown hair

behind her ears

and continued

with her list:

koala: 15kg; Tasmanian

devil: 14kg . . .

"Ruby, it's time to go home now." Mrs
Hanson, Ruby's teacher, came over to
her desk.

Wallaby: 5.5kg; bush-tail possum: 4.5kg;
potoroo: 1.7kg . . . Ruby finished in a rush
and jumped to her feet, worried that Mrs
Hanson might put a hand on her arm.

When people touched her it made her skin feel prickly.

"Did you know there are 235 species of marsupial in Australia? And 334 species in the world?" she asked her teacher.

"No, I didn't," said Mrs Hanson, smiling. "It's clear in the corridor now." She nodded towards where the last few girls were leaving, arms linked, faces close as they chattered about what they were going to do when the summer holidays started. Ruby hated going into the corridor at the end of the school day. She didn't like the way the other kids all talked really loudly and jostled each other as they got their school bags. Mrs

Hanson understood and let her sit and read until everyone had gone.

"Remember to pick up your painting on the way out," Mrs Hanson said. "See you on Monday, Ruby."

Ruby frowned. Her mum had explained that "see you" was just a way of saying goodbye, but it always seemed a weird thing to say. Of course Mrs Hanson would see her on Monday. Why did she feel she had to say it? But she remembered to be polite. "Goodbye," she said and she walked to the corridor.

Through the open door, she could see her mum, wearing shorts and a long floaty top, her dark, wavy hair just touching her shoulders. Ruby collected her painting from where it was drying on the rack and went out into the sunshine, feeling a rush of relief. It was always good to get out of school. She didn't like being surrounded by other kids and having to do what everyone else was doing even when she didn't want to do it. And there were so many rules to remember – not to interrupt people when they were speaking; not to stand too close to people; to say *please* and *thank you* and *sorry*.

"Another new picture?" said Mum, as Ruby reached her. "Hmm . . . let me guess. Is it Cooper?"

"Yes!" said Ruby, beaming, as she showed her the picture. She loved to draw Cooper. He was her dog – a golden retriever with a coat the colour of damp sand, a wagging, feathery tail and melting chocolate-brown eyes.

"Oh, Ruby, it's excellent! It's so like him!" her mum said, taking it. "He looks

just like that when he wants you to
throw his ball for him."

Ruby felt a flush of pride. She'd spent
ages on the picture, carefully sketching
the outline in pencil first and then using
watercolours and a fine brush to add
shading and colour. When she wasn't
reading, she loved to paint. Her pictures
were always very neat and carefully
done with fine lines and watercolours.
She didn't like thick, sticky oil paint.
The feel of it on her skin made her shiver
all over.

"We'll have to put it on the wall," her
mum said. One wall in their kitchen was
covered in a massive pinboard where

Mum and Dad pinned Ruby's best pictures.

"Let's go and put it up now," said Ruby eagerly.

"Soon. We're actually not going home straight away," said Mum.

Ruby frowned. It was Friday, and on Fridays, she and Mum always went straight home and had a snack of apple slices that they dipped in smooth peanut butter. After their snack, Ruby sat at the table and drew while Mum cooked chicken fingers, peas and mashed potato. Dad would come home at six o'clock and they would all sit down to eat together. That was how Fridays worked.

Ruby didn't like things to change. Her voice rose as an anxious knot tightened inside her. "Why aren't we going home?" she demanded. "Why?"

"Don't worry, Ruby," Mum said, in the soothing voice she used when Ruby got stressed over things. "There's no need to be upset. We're not going straight home because we have to call in at Green Gates. That's OK, isn't it?"

Read Baby Koala Rescue to find out what happens next!

Little Orangutan All Alone

Look out for another
great animal story
by Tilda Kelly
coming soon!